1 MONTH OF
FREE
READING

at

www.ForgottenBooks.com

By purchasing this book you are eligible for one month membership to ForgottenBooks.com, giving you unlimited access to our entire collection of over 1,000,000 titles via our web site and mobile apps.

To claim your free month visit:

www.forgottenbooks.com/free567340

ISBN 978-0-484-35185-0
PIBN 10567340

SOPHIA MORTON.

BOSTON,

BOWLES AND DEARBORN, 72 WASHINGTON STREET.

Isaac R. Butts & Co. Printers.
1827.

TO

THE LITTLE GIRL OF EIGHT YEARS

OLD,

FOR WHOM

THIS STORY WAS FIRST WRITTEN,

IT IS NOW

AFFECTIONATELY DEDICATED.

SOPHIA MORTON.

———◆———

"MOTHER, I wonder how you can bear to sit still all day long sewing! I'm sure I am half tired to death with ouly just stitching this one pair of wristbands," said Sophia Morton, as she was folding up her work to put it into her basket; "and I do believe I should die, if I had to be all day poring over stupid shirts, and darning old cotton stockings."

"I try never to be tired of doing what I ought to do, my dear," said her Mother; "and as I am not a little girl like you, perhaps I should not be much hap-

1*

pier, if I were to throw down my work, and jump rope, or dig in the garden with you."

"No, I suppose not, I shouldn't think you would want to play; but you could be reading, Mother, and you could walk and ride, and go abroad, and see company; it would be a great deal pleasanter, I should think, to spend your time so, than in working."

"It would be pleasanter, no doubt, and I do these things sometimes, though not all the time; for how do you think I should like to see your father with his coat out at the elbows, to know that your brother's shirts were in tatters, and his stockings full of holes, while instead of attending to them I had been amusing myself?"

"Oh, but mother, you could get somebody to do such things for you, couldn't you? and besides, I dont see the use for my share, of making such a fuss about clothes. What matter is it how we look, if we only behave well, and are good tempered and obliging? I'm sure there is a great deal more sense, mother, in studying and reading and writing, than there is in spending all your time working over what will wear out the next minute."

"But you know. I do not spend all my time so. I am not *always* working; and would you have people go without clothes entirely?

"Oh, no ma'am, to be sure not; but it is easy to hire people to work for you, there are enough who are glad to do it for their living, and it's very well for them; but I do not see the use of my being obliged to do it. I do hate it worse than any thing else in the world. I wish I could never see a needle and thread again as long as I live; and for my own part, I had rather go in rags, than waste my time so foolishly any more."

"Very well, my dear," said her mother, "we have talked this matter over a great many times before, and I have told you all that can be said about the use and necessity of needle-work ; so I shall say no more, as I see plainly that you are determined not to be convinced. I shall leave you to find out by your own experience, what all the talking in the world will never teach you. Give me your needles and thread, your scissors, thimble, work-basket, and every thing that belongs to it, and I will lock them up, where you shall not be troubled with the sight of them again, until you ask for them."

"Till I ask for them ? Oh dear mother, thank you ! That will be never ; but are you really willing and in earnest, mother ? and will you not be angry with me ?"

"Yes " said her mother, "I am really willing and in earnest, and not in the least angry; but wait before you thank me, and hear all I have to say. Your clothes have been in your own care you know, for more than a year; of course I have nothing to do with them; you must abide by your choice, with all its consequences. No one else shall be allowed to touch them, nor shall I allow you to borrow any of the materials for sewing, of any body. I shall not permit you to do any thing of the kind for me, nor for yourself, until you ask for your basket and return to your old habits."

" Oh, certainly not, ma'am," said Sophia joyfully; " it will be a great while before that time comes I believe. Never work any more! I cannot believe it. Oh dear, how happy, how very happy I shall be."

" We shall see," said her mother, as Sophia put the odious work-basket into her hands; and flew down stairs to tell the joyful news to her brother Julius.

"Only think how much more time I shall have to work in the garden with you, Julius," said she. "My flowers and vegetables will soon look as well as yours, and I shall plant some more strawberries: and then I shall soon get up to you in Làtin, and I will ask papa to let me begin Greek directly. I shall go on as well again, I know, when I don't have to think of leaving off every moment to do that horrid stent."

"Yes, indeed, it is delightful," said Julius, whose contempt for all kinds of girl's work was as great as his sister's; "I am glad you have got rid of all that foolish nonsense at last. So let's make the most of it. I want you to come now and help me plant my border, and then I will go and help you plant yours."

Although Sophia disliked needlework

so much, her mother had alway accustomed her to do it, and as she was thoroughly obedient, she had never neglected any thing she knew she ought to do; therefore her clothes were all now in excellent order. She had not a great many, because as she was growing fast, her mother thought they would be too small for her before she had half worn them out; but they were all nearly new, and perfectly good, and seemed likely to last very well through the summer.

Not long before this time, Mr. and Mrs. Morton had moved into the country, where the children had never lived; and as every thing was new to them they were unusually happy even for them, and seemed hardly able to find words to express their delight and surprise at every thing they saw. After they had satisfied themselves, however with examining every flower in the large garden, and with peeping into every bush and behind every tree in the grove before the house, they were quite willing to return quietly for some hours every day to their studies, as they had always been used to do.

They were both fond of study, and quite forward for their age; and although Julius was two years the oldest, his sister had been able to keep up with him in almost all his studies without much difficulty. They had always studied, read, and played together, except at a particular time every day, when Sophia had been obliged to sit and work with her mother; the only part of her life, in which she was not perfectly happy. She was unhappy, partly because she disliked sewing so much, and partly because it was the only thing in which her brother could not join her. He spent the hours, when she was sewing with her mother, in studying Greek, which she wished very much to learn also. "Now," thought she, "I have nothing else to wish for; I shall never be unhappy again."

They used constantly to work in their little gardens an hour before and another hour after breakfast, and then spend all the rest of the morning in their father's study. He took the whole care of their instruction, and they never were happier than while he was teaching them.

They were very studious, and obedient, and attentive to what was said to them. When by themselves, they behaved as well as while their parents were with them. They were always goodnatured and obliging, always ready to give up to each other in all their plays; to lend each other their playthings, and to help each other in their studies ; so that they gained the entire love of their parents and friends, the servants, and every one who came to the house.

In this manner, the summer was passing quickly away. Sometimes, they received visits from their friends, and then they gave up their own plans for their amusement ; but at other times, they were entirely taken up with their books and their garden ; and Sophia almost forgot that there were any such things as needles and thread in the world. Her stockings often wanted a little mending ; but she thought that was on matter, as the holes were in the feet, where no body could see them. Her frocks, too, began to wear away in sundry places, where she had caught them in the bushes, or tore them in jumping over a fence. A few minutes' work done as soon as the rents were made, would easily have repaired the injury, but this she could not do.

Every time the clothes were washed, they of course became worse and worse; but she would pin the holes together, or tuck them under her belt, so that, as she thought, they would not be observed. "And after all," she would always say to herself or her brother, "what matter is it how I look, if I only behave well?"

Her parents took no notice of all this, for they were resolved to leave her to find out for herself, the consequences of her folly. Her brother was as indifferent about her appearance as as she was herself, and as at this time they had very little company, she was not obliged to think much about it, except while she was dressing.

Every week however brought fresh difficulties. One thing after another, she was absolutely forced to lay aside, which from constant neglect had become unfit to wear. Shoulderstraps, strings and buttons, were continually coming off, and she could hardly make pins supply the places of them all.

Sometimes her skirt hung an inch below her gown, and her gown was hanging loose about her shoulders, the strings off, the belt burst out, and awkwardly pinned together, or perhaps merely *kept* together by her apron.

At last only one common frock remained whole and fit to be seen. It was Monday morning, a beautiful day about the middle of October. Sophia had on this only remaining frock, and was busy in her garden, picking the flower seeds which were just ripening, when Julius came running violently towards her, out of breath, calling out, " Sophia, Sophia, my dear, make haste; come, come quick, here's Uncle and Aunt Howard and all the cousins, a whole carriage full—they are getting out now, come, come quick." Down went the bag of seeds, and away flew Sophia through the walks—up the steps—when just as she reached the last, her foot caught in a tuck that was partly ripped, she fell, and the whole front breadth of the gown was torn quite across. What could she do now? It was impossible for any pinning, even the most judicious, to hide this; she could not, she knew, appear before her aunt in such a condition; and she really had not another frock to put on, excepting one or two thin muslin ones, which, besides being very improper, were much too thin for the season. One of them, however, must answer, and she accordingly dressed herself in it as well as she could, and hoped that nobody would

2*

mind how she looked, or that her dress was quite too fine for the occasion.

She was overjoyed at meeting her cousins, and they were equally glad to see her. They had just returned from a long journey; they had been gone all summer, and had never been at their uncle's new house; so there was every thing to be seen and to be told, on both sides; and Sophia very soon forgot that her dress was any thing but what it should be.

The visiters were impatient to see the garden, and the river, and the grove, of which they had heard so much, in the many letters which had passed between them; and Julius and Sophia were full of the delight of shewing them all the beautiful places which they admired themselves.

They wandered on through the grove, stopping to admire every flower, and to pick every remaining berry, till they forgot that it would ever be time for them to go home. They had reached the farthest extremity of the wood, and were just entering the village, when the sight of the sun just sinking behind a cloud, brought them to their recollections. They turned to go home immediately; Sophia said she was afraid they would be late at tea, and they must walk a little faster, and leave the gleanings of the barberry bushes till to-morrow.

"Yes, I guess you had better walk a little faster," said Melton Howard, the oldest of the cousins; "for it looks to me as if we were going to have a shower; that cloud is coming over very fast, and it looks as black as thunder, and as heavy as lead."

"Well, march on then yourself, and we'll keep up with you," said his older sister, Emily, who had Sophia's ar

" Sophia, my dear, where is your shawl? Didn't you wear any? Nor any bonnet either? I never minded till now, that you were without."

" Oh, I never wear any shawl," said Sophia, "except in the middle of the day, to keep the sun off; in the country, you know, we need'nt mind how we look."

" But I'm afraid you'll take cold, its growing quite cool and damp."

" Oh? never mind Sophia, cousin," said Julius," she never takes cold; since we lived in the country, she is as tough as any of the farmer's daughters, and doesn't mind wind or weather."

"Well, I'm very glad of it, but I'm sure I should catch my death, to be out so late without a shawl; and we must make haste, or I shall as it is; I begin to believe you, Melton, it is going to rain ertainly."—And in truth, though they urried home as fast as possible, they had hardly reached the house, before it poured down tremendously.

Sophia, although Julius declared she never took cold, soon began to find that the sudden change in the weather, together with her thin dress, had been too much for her. She sat shivering all the evening, and could hardly keep comfortable even by the fire. The next morning she awoke with a sore throat, and was so hoarse that she could scarcely speak. She was not sorry for this on the whole, as the excuse of being too unwell to get up, saved her the mortification of going to breakfast in a muslin gown. But after breakfast, her face lengthened, when she heard Julius say that they would all go out chestnutting.

"A chestnutting! Oh that will be grand," said they all at once; " we never picked any chestnuts in our lives;

we shall like to go very much, it will be delightful." "But poor Sophia will have to stay at home," said Melton.

"Never mind that, I can go any time, you know," said she.

"But not with us, cousin," replied Melton; "it will be hardly fair, for us to go away and leave you sick."

"Oh, I'm not very sick yet, and I dare say I shall enjoy myself almost as well at home; I have hardly seen my aunt yet, or looked at the beautiful presents you have brought me."

All the children kindly offered to stay at home with her, but she insisted on being left alone with her mother and aunt, saying that they would enjoy themselves just as well without her, and that she could not be happy, if she thought she was preventing them from the pleasure of chestnutting, which was so new to them all.

They accordingly went without her, and she passed the time slowly but very pleasantly, with her aunt and mother, and the occasional visits of her uncle and father, till two o'clock, when the children all came home.

They burst into the room, with eyes sparkling, all brimfull of some extraordinary matter; so full that they all broke out together, and so loud and fast, that it was impossible for any body to tell one word they were saying. For some time, nothing could be heard but, "Oh, Sophia!" "My dear cousin," "Oh, you don't know what you've lost!" "Oh, if you had only been with us!" "You can't think what a glorious time we've had!" "Oh such a time!" &c. &c.

"What is the matter? do make haste some of you," said Sophia, "and let us know what it is that has happened to you, so very delightful; what has set you into such a fever?"

"I'll tell you cousin," said Louisa, pressing forward, "if the rest will ever let me speak. In the first place you must know we all went into the hill, pasture, as Julius calls it, where the best trees are."

"Yes, yes, I know where it is, and all about that, and I suppose you found the sea-serpent there, or the land dragon."

"How silly! do let me tell you properly; well, we gathered round the trees, Julius and Melton poled them for us, because they were the tallest, and Emily and I—

"Picked away with all your might, at the rate of a gill an hour," interrupted Melton.

Louisa turned her back to him and went on, "they were as thick as they could possibly be. I never saw so many chestnuts together before, and such beauties too, in all my life; we picked a peck I should think—you know it takes so long to get them out of the burrs—when all of a sudden, a great dog sprang out of the bushes, right in amongst us, barking most furiously. I screamed and ran away, and Emily screamed and stood still, and the young gentlemen stood there laughing at us."

"Yes," said Melton, "and well they might ; you would have stood and screamed till this time, I suppose, if it had not been that the dog was more scared than you were, and ran yelping to his master."

"His master? who was his master?" said Sophia.

"I'll tell you, cousin," said Melton. "Louisa was so frightened, that she could'nt see ; but I saw two gentlemen walking in the woods all the time, so I did not believe the dog would eat us up. Well, these gentlemen came up to us, and bowed to Emily, who seemed to be more in her wits, than Louisa, and made a thousand apologies, for their dog being so uncivil as to frighten the young ladies, and drive them away ; and Emily blushed and looked like a fool, and so we all did, till the gentlemen offered to pole the trees, and that made us feel easy. At last they said that we must be tired, and that as their house was only a little way off, we must go in there and rest us. We would not go at first, but they insisted upon it so that at last we could not help it, you know ; so we all marched off, about a quarter of a mile, through the fields, over fences and brooks, till we came to the house."

" And it is a most beautiful place,"

exclaimed Emily; "they carried us into the parlour and introduced us to Mrs. Murray and her sister, (Mr Murray was one of the gentlemen,) and his daughter Cornelia. Sophia, she is the prettiest girl I ever saw. How happens it that you never saw them?"

"Why we have only been here this summer, and they have been gone, ever since we came."

"Yes, now I remember they said so, and how much they wished to be acquainted with you, and my uncle and aunt; and I'm sure I think they are worth being acquainted with, if it were only that one might see such a beautiful place, once in a while. It was as much as I could do, to look first round the room at the handsome furniture, and then out of the window at the fine garden, and orchard and shrubbery. But after we had rested us a little, Mrs.

Murray asked Miss Cornelia if she would show us her play-room; she smiled, and asked me if I would like to go. I was sorry at first that they should think

amused with play-things; but I thought it would not be civil to refuse, so we went; and I found that the gentlemen and ladies were following us.

"Walk up, walk up young gentleman," they said to the boys, who hung back as if they were half ashamed, "you need not be ashamed to venture into such a play-room as Cornelia's; I dare say you will find something that will entertain you."

"And so we did indeed, mother;" said Julius, who had long been impatient for his turn to speak; "but first we passed through several very handsome rooms, all hung round with paintings, which I wanted to stop and look

at, and then through a noble library,
which I just longed to overhaul, and
then we got to the play-room. It was
a very large room, and the first things
we saw were all kinds of games, such
as swings, battledores, coronella, jump-
ropes, backgammon and chessboards,
and a great many others we never saw
before. While we were looking over
these, I observed for the first time, that
the room was circular, and that it
was completely surrounded by one im-
mense painting. Mr. Murray told
us that it was a Panorama of the
world. He went up to it with us, and
explained the whole. It was divi-
ded into four parts, one for each quarter of the globe, and in each quarter
there were a great many separate
paintings, representing all the natural
curiosities, the manners and customs,
and national dresses of the inhabitants

3*

of each particular nation, and the re-
markable animals, and every thing that
is worth knowing of every country; I
mean every thing that can be put into
a picture. I am sure l could learn more
Geography there in one day, than by
studying a whole year out of a book.
I mean I could have a better idea of
the manners and customs of the people of the different countries; I should
feel better acquainted with them."

All the children now broke in, and
began to describe to whomever would
hear them, what each one remembered
and liked best. One told about the
North American Indian women carry-
ing their children on their backs, and
of the elks and buffaloes roaming
through the forests, with the Indian
hunters pursuing them; and another
told about the Hindoo woman, burning
herself on the funeral pile of her hus-

band, and of the battle between the tiger and the Boa, a huge serpent who winds himself round the tiger and crushes him to death. Melton described the bull-fights of Spain; Louisa the pretty picture of the French vine-dressers. It seemed as if they could not be tired of telling how much they had enjoyed.

"I am sure, mother," said Melton Howard, "I know, aunt, you would say it was the most beautiful and ingenions thing, you ever saw. I did not see half I wanted to, after all, and I believe we should have stayed there a week, if it had not been for Emily."

"Oh, Emily didn't care half so much about seeing it as we did," said Louisa; "she was listening to what the gentlemen and ladies were saying. I didn't understand it, nor care any thing about it."

" But you would if you had listened, Louisa. Mr. Murray was telling the other gentleman, Mr. Powel, I believe his name is, how he came by this beautiful Panorama. He had it made in France. He has just come from France, I believe. He had been acquainted, when he was there before, with a young painter named Brouchet; he was a very industrious man, but very unfortunate. He was married and had been going on very well, till by some accident, he lost all he was worth in the world ; and when Mr. Murray found him out this last time, he was almost starving. Mr. Murray wanted to give him some money, but he was too proud to take it; he said he was able to work and would work gladly ; if he could get no employment, he would starve; but he could never eat the bread of idleness. Mr. Murray said that he then tried to get some employment for him, but he could not. At last he thought. the plan of this Panorama; he desc. bed it to Mr. Brouchet, and he told him he thought he could do it without any difficulty. Mr. Murray paid him as he went along, so that it saved him completely; and set him up again in business, at once. Every body flocked to see this curious piece of work, and were so much pleased with it, that he soon had as much work as he could possibly do. That was the right way of being generous, wasn't it, mother?"

"Yes, my son; as he could afford it so well, it was certainly the most generous thing he could have done, and it did the young man more good than twice the sum of money would have done. There is no way of doing so much good to the poor, and with so much certainty too, as to give them employment."

This morning's amusement gave the children something to talk about through the rest of the visit, which lasted till the next morning. They repeated over and over again, as children always do, all they had seen and heard.

Sophia could hardly conceal her vexation; but as long as she could throw the blame of her disappointment upon any thing else, she was resolved not to give up her foolish resolution, which was the real cause of it.

Soon after. this time, the weather, which had been as warm as summer, became much cooler, and showed that autumn had really come, and that winter was fast approaching.

Sophia now found her thin frocks very uncomfortable. She tried on those which she had worn the last winter, but she had grown so much that they were quite too small; the sleeves were far above her wrists, and the belt would not meet, leaving a wide open seam behind. She was really not fit to be seen; and although her brother said all he could to persuade her, "that it would do very well, and that it was of no sort of consequence how she looked if she only behaved well, and that she was the best scholar of her age any where;"—still she could not help feeling ashamed of herself, and kept entirely out of sight, if there was any danger of being seen by strangers. She shut herself up with her books in her father's study, and while she was reading or studying she forgot her troubles, and was perfectly happy.

As the winter approached, however, and she was deprived of the pleasure of working in her garden, she was some-

times at a loss for some employment.
Fond as she was of her books, she could
not be always reading; to do nothing
else all day long and all the evening,
became tiresome even to her. Her
brother had many amusements out of
doors, in which she could not always
join; these took him away from her,
during some hours of every day. And
there was one thing which troubled her
more than all the rest; she could not
now, as she used to do, spend any of
the time with her mother. Her mother never allowed her to be for a moment idle; if she was with her, she must
be employed. But what could she do?
She tried in vain to think of something;
there was nothing but to read, and if
she did read, it deprived her of what
she wanted most, her mother's pleasant
conversation. For she always contrived to make every thing pleasant, even
her instructions.

Sophia thought of all these things, more and more every day. She was fairly tired of looking like a slut, and she might at this time have been easily brought to return to her duty, if it had not been for the constant entreaties of her brother. He begged her not " to be so foolish as to give up, and be just like all other girls, caring for nothing but dress and such nonsense.—Mother is perfectly willing you should do as you please, dear Sophia," he would say; " then why need you think of any thing else ?"

An event happened about this time, which soon determined her what to do.

She was one morning sitting at her studies as usual, when a carriage drove to the door, and she saw two ladies and a girl about her own age, whom she did not know, alight from it.

It was not long before the servant came, to call her down into the parlor.

"Who are those ladies, Nancy?" said Sophia.

"I don't know ma'am, but they are mighty smart folks, and they asked for you, and your mamma says that you must come down."

"I can't go down, Nancy.   I don't look fit to see any body, I'm sure.   My gown doesn't meet behind, and my vandyke won't half cover it, and it's above my ancles, though I let down a welt this morning.   I can't go down; what shall I do?"

"Why I don't know, ma'am, I'm sure," said Nancy : " if there was time, I don't know but I could fix your gown so that it would do; or if you'd just let me step into your room and fix one of your others——"

"Oh, no," said Sophia; " mamma

has forbidden that any body should do any thing for me, and I cannot disobey her."

" But, Miss Sophia, I will never tell her, she'll never know it; only just let me set a stitch——"

" Nancy, for shame. How, can you try to make me deceive my mother? Go down to her, and tell her I cannot come."

Nancy left the room with this message very unwillingly ; and Sophia sat down again to her books, more sad, and more vexed with herself, than ever.

" Well Sophia," said her mother, when she went to dinner, " you have lost a great deal by your studying fit, this morning.—Mrs. Murray and her daughter made me a very long, pleasant visit. I like them very much. They have left an invitation, for you and

Julius, to a little dance at their house, tomorrow evening."

"Tomorrow evening! a dance!" said both the children, "oh delightful! And may we go, mother?"

"Yes, I promised Mrs. Murray that you should both go. They are to send a carriage for you, at half past four; so remember to be ready."

"Yes, yes, we shall be ready, mother, no fear of that. I would not miss seeing that beautiful place again for any thing," said Julius.

Poor Sophia found it no very easy matter to get her dress in readiness. But something must be contrived. She took every article of her clothes out of her drawers and laid them on the bed, that she might choose from among them, what would suit her purpose best.

First, she selected a beautiful dotted

India muslin. This was in a better condition, than any other frock she had. The belt was a good deal worn with pinning, for the hooks and eyes had burst off, and the string at the top of the waist behind, was broken out; it was a full waist, and pinning it, gave it a most untidy appearance. But she had a broad blue sash, and this she thought she could put on by crossing it behind, so as *almost* to hide both these defects.

The skirt which she usually wore with this dress—it was a nice cambric —had been a little torn behind. A moment's work would have mended it, but it was left from week to week, every day adding a little to the length of the rent, till now it was slit from top to bottom. She must therefore wear a coarser one ; but she hoped that nobody would mind it, and that the holes in it would not show through her gown.

I cannot tell how much difficulty she had with every article she took hold of, in contriving ways of hiding little defects, that met her eye wherever she turned it; nothing was exactly as it should be, and she was tempted many times to give up in despair.

"But if I only had a needle and thread," said she to herself, "how easily all these things could be put to rights. Ah, dear mother, if you did but know how miserable I feel at this moment, I am sure you would pity me; perhaps you would forgive me; for I know now, that I have been doing wrong. I will go to her this moment, and ask her to forgive me. But no; she will think it is only because I want to appear a little better at this party; she will not believe that I am really convinced of my folly. I will wait till this is over, and then I will— yes, I certainly will ask her for my work basket."

At half past four precisely, the children were dressed and waiting for the carriage. Sophia looked round for her mother, for she always wanted to see whether she was properly dressed, before going away on a visit. Her mother was not to be found, though she searched all over the house and garden; and she had just given up the hope of finding her, when the carriage came to the door. They both jumped in, and rode off in fine spirits.

Sophia was quite as much delighted with Mr. Murray's house, and especially with the play-room, as she expected to be, and that is saying a great deal. She had been sent for early, that she might see it as much as she wished, before the other children came. Cornelia Murray was very kind to her, showed her every thing which she thought would entertain her, and was so good natured and obliging, that Sophia began to love her very much, and was almost sorry that any other children were coming.

After tea, however, they all came, and were carried into a large room without a carpet, where a boy with a violin was waiting to play for them to dance.

Sophia seated herself among the little girls, some of whom she had not seen for a great while, and began to talk to them. She was surprised to find that they all for some reason tried to avoid speaking to her, and seemed unwilling to have any thing to do with her, or even to sit by her.

One after another, they got up and

walked across the room, where they all stood talking together, very busily. They often looked toward the place where Sophia was sitting, and laughed; and she could not help thinking that they must be laughing at her. Before she decided about it, however, Cornelia's mother came and sat down by her, and talked for some time with her; so she thought no more about it.

Meantime the dancing began. Sophia was very fond of dancing, but one cotillion and another were finished, and nobody came to ask her, though she well remembered that at dancing school, she was always among the first to be taken out.

Mrs. Murray at last took pity upon her, and asked her to dance with her, which she was very glad to do. But she was so much vexed by the neglect of her companions, that she could do nothing well; she made many awkward mistakes, and though she knew the figures perfectly well, she often disturbed the whole set.

When she sat down, Mrs. Murray was obliged to leave her, and was soon afterwards called out of the room.

Sophia was sitting alone near the fire, and a large party of girls, who happened not to be dancing, stood round it, laughing and talking very loud, so loud, that she could not help hearing what they said.

" Did you ever see such a figure ?" —" How shabby !" " How sluttish !" " Should'nt you be ashamed to go abroad looking so ?" " I wonder what Mrs. Murray thinks !" were sentences she heard repeated, till she was sure they could mean nobody but herself; especially as some of the smaller girls would occasionally take a sly peep at her.

" Yes, I'm sure I should be ashamed to go into our kitchen in such a dress as that ;" said one of the older girls— " Do look, Lucy Ropes! I wonder if she thinks her fine dotted muslin hides her ragged petticoat ?"   .

" Or if her nice pink slippers cover· all the holes in her famous silk stockings ! I should rather wear good cotton ones for my share ; there's a hole in the heel, I saw it when she was dancing, did'nt you, Miss Barclay ? It was as big as the palm of your hand ; I saw the boys laugh at that, did'nt you ?"

" Yes, indeed, they laughed well at her and her ragged finery,", said Miss Barclay. " And her gloves too, did you see them ? there is a rip in every one of the fingers, and they are torn half way up the arm besides."

4*

" Oh, did you hear what the boys said about her tucker ? See ! her beautiful Mechlin lace, is hanging half off her neck, and William Chatterton said

only meant to be *tucked* on !"

The girls all laughed loud and long at this witty speech, and then they began to whisper together.

At last, Miss Barclay's voice was heard above the rest, " I tell you I will go, I declare I will. Come along, Lucy—we'll have some fun."

" Oh, how can you be so rude," said some of the little girls. " Miss Barclay ! Lucy Ropes ! Don't, pray don't ! For mercy's sake."

" For mercy's sake ! Do hold your tongues, girls ; just as if I don't know what I'm about. I say I will go, stop me if you dare !" said Miss Barclay, breaking away from them, for they had caught fast hold of her hands and her gown.

She sat down quietly by Sophia, with Lucy Ropes on the other side, and began talking to her very pleasantly about the dancing, the rooms, Cornelia, and the rest of the young ladies. At last she began with, " What a beautiful dress you have on, Miss Morton ; how sweetly it sets, especially behind ! Who made it ? Do just turn round, and let me see how the back is cut. This is quite a new fashion, I declare, is'nt it Lucy ? Pray Miss Morton, do you mend your clothes yourself, or do you keep a maid on purpose ? I hate to mend of all things, don't you ? I always wear my clothes till they come to mending, and then I give them away, and get new ones."

" I hate to see any thing after it's mended," said Lucy ; " I had rather wear my clothes in rags, hadn't you, Anna?"

"Miss Morton, where do you buy your gloves?" said Anna Barclay, taking hold of her hand, so as to display all the holes to the greatest advantage; "Oh, I suppose you got them of Mrs. Noah, who lives in Ark-Row. Did you buy them before the flood, or after?"

Here the little girls, who one by one had gathered round to hear what was going on, burst out into loud and re-

young lady ran on in the same strain, trying every means to keep them laughing, and to torment poor Sophia as much as possible.

How long she would have gone on, I cannot tell; but at last, when it seemed as if the poor child could bear no more, Mrs. Murray, who had but just perceived what was going on, looked over the heads of the little troop, and fixing her eyes upon Miss Barclay, said in a most severe tone, " Young ladies, it is time for you to leave off this game ; come down to supper !"

These words, and still more the severe look which Mrs. Murray gave as she said them, sobered the whole party instantly ; and they looked very much ashamed, when taking Sophia kindly by the hand, she said, " You shall come with me, my dear ; I can love a sweet tempered, modest little girl, even if she has behaved foolishly : and I am much more disposed to pardon her folly, which I am sure she will soon correct, than the folly of those who have been trying to torment her, because she happens for once not to be dressed as neatly as she ought to be."

Sophia had borne all the cruel mockery of her companions, without saying a single word, to excuse herself or to provoke them; but as soon as she heard the kind words of Mrs. Murray, and felt that she should be forgiven, she burst into tears; and taking her hand, she entreated to be sent immediately home, begging Mrs. Murray to spare her the shame of sitting down to supper with those young ladies.

Her request was instantly granted. Mrs. Murray ordered the carriage, and sent Cornelia to bid her good night.

Cornelia ran to her, threw her arms round her neck and kissed her, and then told her how sorry she was that she had been so rudely treated. She said it was as much as she could do, to keep her promise of not speaking to her all the evening.

"Who made you promise that," said Sophia.

"I can't tell you now," replied Cornelia; "don't ask me. I dare say you will know all about it soon. Good night, dear Sophia, I'm sure I shall love you very much."

As soon as they got into the carriage, the children both exclaimed at once, " Oh, brother," " oh, sister," "what an evening we have spent! How different from what we expected!" " Oh, how foolishly, how wrong, I have acted!" said Sophia.

" Not any worse than I have, dear sister," said Julius; " I encouraged you, I told you to keep on. If it hadn't been for me, I don't believe you could have held out so long. But I'm sure I have been well punished, by what I have suffered to night, and what I saw you were suffering. I won't tell you all I heard—"

"Oh yes, dear Julius, do tell me; you ought to indeed, I ought to know every word, and it cannot be worse than what I heard myself."

"You don't know, and I didn't know myself till to night, how boys will talk; they said a great many things about you that I would not tell you for the world." "But you must tell me some of them at least: what were they?"

"Why, they all said they wouldn't dance with such a sluttish looking girl; and they all laughed at you. One boy said he wouldn't touch such ragged gloves; and another said he never knew a girl before, who went to balls with holes in her stockings. Some said you had better learn to darn them, than to stuff yourself with so much 'Greek and Hebrew, which were only proper for boys. And then they all began to laugh at your being so fond of study · and that made me angry, because you know that is right, though I do think

now, it is wrong to neglect other things
so much. I didn't know before that
you would be so much laughed at for
it."

"Well, I am glad we know it now,"
said Sophia, drying her eyes; "I believe I shall be better for it as long as I
live."

"But the worst thing of all I havn't
told you yet," said Julius. "I happened to be standing behind a door,
and Mrs. Murray and an old gentleman
came and stood before it, so that I
could not get out, and they could not
see me. And I heard the gentleman
ask Mrs. Murray who that little girl
was, with a broad blue sash, sitting
alone? 'It's a pity she's so untidy,'
said he; 'she would be a very pretty
girl, if it were not for that.'

"'She is a very sensible little girl,'
Mrs. Murray said, 'and a fine scholar

besides.' I loved her, for saying that,' but the gentleman went on. 'So much the worse, ma'am, so much the worse. I hate to see girls brought up to care for nothing but books. It wasn't so in my day, ma'am; then the girls had to mend their own stockings and sew their own gowns, and leave Latin and Greek, and such nonsense to their brothers and husbands. I can tell you, ma'am, they looked a great deal better than that shabby little lady, with all her book knowledge.'

" ' Would you have girls care for nothing but dress then,' said Mrs. Murray, 'and grow up ignorant, and vain, and foolish?'

" ' Why, not quite so bad as that,' the gentleman said. 'They ought to be taught to read, of course; but they are

they have a little smattering of one

thing and another, than if they did not pretend to go beyond their sampler and their spelling book.'

" ' There I agree with you,' said Mrs. Murray, 'if they have only a little smattering. They must know a great deal, or else, as you say, they had better know nothing. Enough at least should be taught them, to make them feel that though they may study forever, there will still be an abundance left to learn. And this may be easily done, without neglecting any thing else of real consequence.'

" ' That's very true, ma'am, very true,' said the gentleman ; 'but you don't uphold this young lady, I take it, in neglecting every thing else for the sake of her books? But what sort of a woman is her mother? Perhaps I have blamed this poor girl too much, after all ; it may be that her mother does not take proper care of her. She may be a very odd woman, and perhaps not very clever.'

" ' No, that is unjust,' said **Mrs.** Murray ; ' the mother of this chlld is a very excellent woman, though people will be ready to blame her for the fault of her daughter. She told me that · her daughter had taken a great dislike to needle work, and that she had forbidden her to do it, in order that by suffering for the want of it, she might learn its value. She suffered her to come here in this improper dress, and requested my daughter not to take any notice of her, but leave her to the mercy of her little friends, that she might find out by experience, that her conduct would certainly expose her to ridicule. It is an experiment you see, but I think it will succeed.' "

" Only think, brother, how **dreadful**

it is," said Sophia, "to bring disgrace
upon our dear mother, as well as on
myself; for though Mrs. Murray told
that gentleman how it was, other people will think as he did, and there will
be nobody to correct them."

"Oh, it's all horrid, I know," replied
Julius, "I can't bear to think of it; but
I must just tell you, that this gentleman
went on talking about it for some time.
Then he told Mrs. Murray how fond
he was of young people, and finished
by asking her to invite the children that
were there to night to a dance at his
house a month from this time. 'All,'
said he, 'except that young lady with
the great sash. I can't have her, it
would spoil all my pleasure, unless you
can bring me word that she has reformed; then I shall be more glad to
see her than any of the rest.'"

When they reached home, they went

immediately in search of their mother. They found her alone in the parlor, waiting for them. Sophia could not speak. She threw herself sobbing into her mother's arms, and as soon as her tears would let her, asked her forgiveness.

"Indeed, mother," said Julius, "I think she has been punished enough; especially as it was partly my fault. She would not have been so much to blame, if it had not been for me."

He then related all that had happened through the evening, and ended with saying, "Oh, she has been punished enough, and more than all the rest, by what we never thought of before, that the blame would be thrown upon you."

"I have no thought of punishing either of you, my children," said Mrs. Morton. "You have indeed punished yourselves, and that very severely. It is a harsh lesson, but it is one which I could not have taught you so thoroughly in any other way; and I think that you will neither of you ever forget it. I can assure you, that I have suffered quite as much as you have, and I could not have kept my resolution, but for the hope that it would be a lasting benefit to you.

"You will one of these days, my daughter," continued she, turning to Sophia, "become a woman; and you will then discern, better than you can now, how happy you were to have been taught and to have practised when you were young, all those things which every woman ought to know, and without which she can never be either respected or happy. Let her be ever so learned or so wise, she will always be laughed at, if she is found to be ignorant of them. But this, I hope,

will never be the case again with my
daughter."

"Never, dear mother; I shall never
be so foolish again, I am sure; and I

been to me, and how much you have
suffered for me. I can not do any
thing to reward you; but I am sure
that I will never do any thing, as long
as I live, which I know will make you
unhappy."

———

I am happy to inform those of my
little readers who wish to know what
became of Sophia Morton, that she
kept this resolution faithfully; and that
at the end of the month, she and her
brother were particularly invited to the
house of the old gentleman, who had
declared it would spoil all his pleasure
to see such an untidy little girl in his
house. He had learned from Mrs.

Murray that she had reformed, and he was as much pleased with her appearance on this evening, as he had formerly been disgusted.

CPSIA information can be obtained
at www.ICGtesting.com
Printed in the USA
BVHW04*1239140918
527538BV00007B/475/P